Fairy *

to You *

Annie Ulbrich

FAIRY TEA

BY
ANNIE ULLRICH

ILLUSTRATED BY
JENA RAWLEY-WHITAKER

WINDOM BOOKS

GRANDPA GREEN WAS EVERY CHILD'S DREAM.
TAP DANCE WAS HIS TRADE,
GARDENING HIS LOVE. MISCHIEF DANCED
IN HIS EYES. HE ALWAYS WORE
A SHAMROCK.

Pansy

BUT EVEN HE COULD NOT SAVE
KRISTEN & ALLIE FROM
AUNTIE BLUE AND NANA GREEN'S
BRIDGE PARTY.

Fuchsia

TOO MANY HANDS TO
SHAKE AND CURTSIES TO MAKE,
AND ONE HAD TO
STAND UP STRAIGHT,.....OR.....

Lisianthus

.....BE BANISHED
TO THE HORSEHAIR SOFA.

"THIS PETTICOAT SCRATCHES."
"MY FINGERS ARE HOT."
"OH MY," ALLIE POUTED.

KRISTEN THREW HER A DIRTY LOOK..
ALLIE WAS ALWAYS SAYING "OH MY,"
AND KRISTEN WAS TIRED OF IT.

Pink

KRISTEN SAW HER CHANCE
AND SNUCK OUTSIDE.
ALLIE FOLLOWED.

Cyclamen

THE NANAS LOVED
GOSSIP AND GARDENING. THEIR PARTY
BLOOMED WITH CHATTER.
"YOUNG LADIES," NANA GREEN CALLED. "DON'T GET
YOUR DRESSES DIRTY."

· Fairy Rose ·

KRISTEN CURTSIED. ALLIE DID
A QUICK DIP.
"NOW DON'T GET INTO ANY TROUBLE,"
NANA CAUTIONED.
TROUBLE WAS JUST WHAT KRISTEN
WAS LOOKING FOR.

· *Foxglove* ·

SOON THEY WERE OUT OF SIGHT
OF THE HOUSE.
ALLIE STARED DOWN THE LONG, NARROW
PATH AND REFUSED TO MOVE.
"COME ON," KRISTEN YANKED.

• Marigold •

ALLIE DUG IN HER HEELS.
KRISTEN PULLED HARDER UNTIL
ALLIE CAME FLYING -

· *Iris* ·

- AND LANDED, PLOP,
IN THE MUD.
"NOW SEE WHAT YOU'VE DONE,"
ALLIE WAILED. "OH MY! I
WANTED TO STAY CLEAN AND NEAT
FOR NANA."
"SHHHH....." KRISTEN SAID.
"DID YOU HEAR THAT?"

• *Freesia* •

ALLIE STOPPED SNIFFLING.
"GRANDPA GREEN!"
KRISTEN NODDED. "HE MUST BE AT THE OTHER
END OF THE GARDEN."

· English Ivy ·

ROUND AND ROUND THEY WOUND.
THE FARTHER THE PATH WENT,
THE CLOSER, DARKER, AND MORE LUSH
THE GARDEN BECAME.
THEY HAD NEVER BEEN SO FAR BY THEMSELVES.
JUST WHEN THEY WERE ABOUT TO GIVE UP, A MAGICAL VOICE WHISPERED:

Pink

"REMEMBER, THERE ARE FAIRIES AT
THE BOTTOM OF THE GARDEN."
"FAIRIES!"
KRISTEN CHECKED BEHIND EVERY ROCK.
ALLIE PEEKED UNDER EACH LEAF.
FAIRIES!

Cosmos .

SUDDENLY, KRISTEN STOPPED SO ABRUPTLY
THAT - BUMP - ALLIE RAN INTO HER
AND TUMBLED BACKWARDS.
"OH MY!" ALLIE CRIED, BUT KRISTEN
MOTIONED FOR HER TO BE QUIET.

· *Poppy* ·

THERE, IN A CLEARING WHICH
KRISTEN WAS QUITE CERTAIN
HAD NEVER BEEN THERE BEFORE,
SAT A TEA SET JUST THEIR SIZE.

Anemone

Pour some
tea
and
the fairies
will come!

ALLIE SQUEALED AND
RAN FOR THE FOOD.
KRISTEN STEPPED FORWARD CAUTIOUSLY
AND PICKED UP A NOTE.
A SHAMROCK FLOATED TO THE GROUND.

· Mint ·

ALLIE & KRISTEN SAT DOWN TO POUR,
BUT THERE WERE NO CUPS FOR THE FAIRIES.
BEFORE ALLIE COULD COMPLAIN,
KRISTEN SPIED
AN ACORN CAP.
"QUICK," SHE COMMANDED AND
THEY SCURRIED LIKE SQUIRRELS FOR MORE.
THEN THEY LINED UP THE CAPS AND
KRISTEN POURED A SPOT OF TEA INTO EACH ONE.

Thimbleflower

ALLIE REACHED FOR A TEA CAKE. KRISTEN FROWNED.
"WHERE ARE YOUR MANNERS?"
"OH MY," ALLIE SIGHED.
THEY WAITED, BUT NO FAIRIES CAME.

Bleeding

"TWEEEEEEE..." SOUNDED A WHISTLE,
SOFT & LIGHTER THAN THE WIND.
A GENTLE BREEZE TICKLED THEIR EARS.

Heart

THEN ALLIE KNEW.
FAIRIES WEREN'T IN TREES OR UNDER ROCKS.
FAIRIES WERE HIDDEN
IN THE GRASS.
SHE THREW HERSELF DOWN,
WHITE DRESS AND ALL. CAREFULLY SHE
PARTED THE REEDS.

Scarlet Paintbrush

THERE, AMID BLUEBELLS AND DAFFODILS,
WITH MORNING GLORY UMBRELLAS
AND LILY PAD SEATS,
SAT A CIRCLE OF FAIRIES.
"COME JOIN US," THEY WAVED.
THEY PROFFERED
BUTTERFLY CAKES ON SHAMROCK PLATES.
THEY SIPPED BLUEBERRY DEW
IN BLUEBELL BOWLS.

· *Ram's Horn* ·

ALLIE RAN BACK TO GET MORE TEA.
THIS TIME SHE POURED AND DID NOT SPILL ONE DROP.

· *False Dragonhead* ·

AFTER TEA, THE FAIRIES AND THE GIRLS TALKED.
THE FAIRIES WERE LIGHT AS A KISS IN KRISTEN'S HAND.

Star Grass

THEY TOLD SECRETS
AND SANG SONGS.

Alba

"BUTTERFLY BREEZES AND
DRAGONFLY DAYS
RAINDROP RAINBOWS AND
BRIGHT SUMMER RAYS."

Tickclover

"WE DANCE IN A CIRCLE
WARMED BY THE SUN
ALIVE WITH ADVENTURE,
LAUGHTER AND FUN."

· Gentian ·

KRISTEN & ALLIE DANCED AND SANG.
THEY FLOWERED WITH LOVE, LIGHT & JOY
UNTIL, EXHAUSTED, THEY FELL ASLEEP.

Wood Sorrel

SOFTLY THE FAIRIES FANNED THE
CHILDREN'S FOREHEADS.
GENTLY SWEET-SCENTED PETALS DRIFTED
ONTO WEARY LITTLE HEADS.

Lady's Slipper

THERE WAS A PEACE LIKE THE GARDEN
HAD NEVER KNOWN.

Rose Hips

"KRISTEN ELIZABETH! ALLIE ANN!
A VOICE BOOMED FROM THE HOUSE.
KRISTEN JOLTED UP.
SHE TURNED TO THE FAIRIES,
BUT THEY AND THE TEA WERE GONE.

French Mulberry

"GIRLS! COME INSIDE!
IT'S TIME TO SAY GOOD-BY TO OUR GUESTS."
THE COMMANDING VOICE TRAILED
DOWN THE HILL.

· *Rhododendron* ·

DUSTING THE GRASS OFF THEIR DRESSES,
THE TWO GIRLS RACED UP THE PATH
AS FAST
AS THEIR DRESS SHOES WOULD CARRY THEM.

· Bluebells ·

"WHERE HAVE YOU BEEN?" NANA ASKED,
EYING THE GRASS STAINS & MUD.
"AT THE BOTTOM OF THE GARDEN," ALLIE CONFESSED.
"THERE ARE FAIRIES THERE, NANA."
"FAIRIES! AHK, YOU'VE BEEN LISTENING TO
TOO MANY OF GRANDPA GREEN'S STORIES."
"BUT, - " PROTESTED ALLIE.
"NOW INSIDE," NANA INSISTED,
LIFTING FLOWERS OUT OF ALLIE'S HAIR.

Miniature Rosa "Cupcake"

RELUCTANTLY THE GIRLS STEPPED INTO THE PARLOR.
A WHISTLE SOUNDED.
THEY TURNED FOR ONE LAST LOOK.
THERE STOOD GRANDPA GREEN & CANARY THE CAT.

Lilium

HE NODDED TOWARD THE LILIES,
"SHHHH...." KRISTEN SMILED.
"THERE <u>ARE</u> FAIRIES AT THE BOTTOM OF THE GARDEN."
ALLIE WHISPERED.

"Journey's End"

GRANDPA GREEN SMILED BACK
AND THEN, WITH A WAVE OF HIS HOE,
A WHISTLE, AND A WINK, HE WAS GONE.

· *Columbine* ·

NANA'S KITCHEN RULES

1. START WITH A CLEAN AND TIDY KITCHEN.

2. WASH YOUR HANDS.

3. WEAR AN APRON OR PINAFORE
   TO KEEP YOUR CLOTHES CLEAN.

4. READ THE RECIPE ALL THE WAY THROUGH
   BEFORE STARTING.
   GATHER ALL THE INGREDIENTS TOGETHER FIRST.

5. FOLLOW DIRECTIONS VERY CAREFULLY.
   DO EXACTLY WHAT THE RECIPE TELLS YOU TO DO.

6. DON'T HURRY. TAKE YOUR TIME.

7. CLEAN AND TIDY UP THE KITCHEN WHEN
   YOU ARE DONE. LEAVE IT AS YOU FOUND IT.

ALWAYS HAVE AN ADULT
ASSIST YOU IN THE KITCHEN
ESPECIALLY WHEN BOILING OR
COOKING ON THE STOVE.

FAIRY CAKES

MAKES 3 DOZEN MINIATURE TEACAKES

1 STICK BUTTER OR MARGARINE
2/3 CUP SUGAR
2 EGGS
1/4 CUP MILK
1 1/4 CUP SELF-RISING FLOUR
PINCH OF SALT
1/2 CUP GROUND ALMONDS
1/2 CUP FRESH OR FROZEN BLUEBERRIES
BLUEBERRIES (OR OTHER FRESH BERRIES)
& MINT LEAVES FOR GARNISH

CREAM THE BUTTER OR MARGARINE WITH THE SUGAR
UNTIL LIGHT AND FLUFFY.

WHISK IN THE 2 EGGS (BEATEN).

ADD FLOUR, SALT, AND THE GROUND NUTS.

THE BATTER WILL BE STIFF. (ADD A LITTLE MILK IF NEEDED.)
CAREFULLY STIR IN THE BLUEBERRIES.

GREASE MINIATURE MUFFIN PANS. FILL EACH 2/3 FULL.

BAKE FOR 16-18 MINUTES AT 400 DEGREES.

WHEN GOLDEN, REMOVE FROM OVEN AND COOL.
REMOVE FROM PAN.

SPRINKLE LIBERALLY WITH FAIRY DUST.
TOP EACH LITTLE TEA CAKE WITH
A BLUEBERRY & 2 SMALL MINT LEAVES.

FOR ADDED FESTIVITY:

WRAP EACH CAKE IN A DOILY
&
TIE WITH A THIN RIBBON
OR
BAKE IN MINIATURE GOLD FOIL
CUPCAKE PAPERS

FAIRY TEA

4 CUPS FRESH WATER
        BROUGHT TO A ROLLING BOIL
3 TEASPOONS OF YOUR FAVORITE LOOSE TEA
        (OR 3 BAGS IF YOU PREFER)
2 TABLESPOONS HONEY OR SUGAR
1 CUP WARMED MILK

PLACE TEA IN A CLEAN, WARM TEA POT.
ADD BOILING WATER AND HONEY OR SUGAR.
LET THIS STAND FOR 3-5 MINUTES, THEN ADD WARM MILK.
POUR INTO SMALL TEA CUPS AND SERVE.

ONLY CHILDREN ARE ALLOWED TO DRINK FAIRY TEA

FAIRY DUST

1-2 TABLESPOONS POWDERED SUGAR
1 SMALL TEA STRAINER OR SIEVE

PUT A SPOONFUL OF POWDERED SUGAR IN SIEVE.
SHAKE OVER COOKIES, CAKES, OR EVEN
        OVER YOUR CUP OF TEA BEFORE DRINKING.

FAIRY DUST INFUSES TEA WITH FAIRY MAGIC.

BUTTERFLY CAKES

MAKES 7-9 CAKES THE SIZE OF A TEA CUP

6 TABLESPOONS BUTTER OR MARGARINE
1/3 CUP SUGAR
1/4 TEASPOON VANILLA
1 EGG
1 CUP SELF-RISING FLOUR, SIFTED
PINCH OF SALT
MILK (APPROXIMATELY 1/4 CUP)
JAM — YOUR FAVORITE KIND
WHIPPED CREAM
CANDIED ORANGE OR FRUIT SLICES
          (OR FRESH TANGERINE SLICES)

CREAM TOGETHER THE BUTTER AND SUGAR.
BEAT IN THE EGG AND VANILLA.
STIR IN HALF THE FLOUR AND ADD THE PINCH OF SALT.
ADD A LITTLE MILK AND THE REMAINING FLOUR.
     THE BATTER SHOULD BE SOFT.*
          (* ADD THE REST OF THE MILK IF NECESSARY.)
LINE CUPCAKE TINS WITH CUPCAKE PAPERS. FILL THE CUPS 2/3 FULL.
BAKE FOR 20-25 MINUTES AT 375 DEGREES.
WHEN A NICE, LIGHT BROWN, REMOVE AND
     LET THE PAN COOL ON A WIRE RACK.

TO MAKE WINGS:

USE A SPOON & DIG A HOLE 2/3 DEEP
IN THE CENTER OF EACH CAKE.
FILL THE HOLE WITH JAM.
SPREAD WHIPPED CREAM OVER THE TOP OF THE JAM,
SO THE CAKE IS ICED LIKE A CLOUD.
ANGLE TWO CANDIED FRUIT SLICES IN A "V" ON TOP.
USE A BERRY OR SMALLER PIECE OF CANDIED FRUIT
FOR THE BUTTERFLY'S HEAD.

SPRINKLE WITH FAIRY DUST.

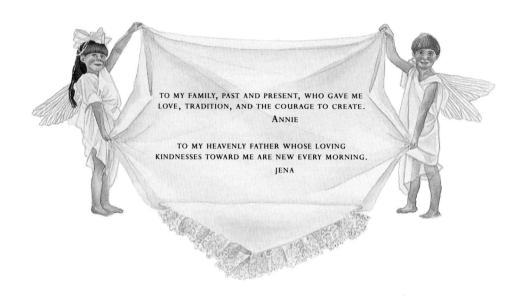

TO MY FAMILY, PAST AND PRESENT, WHO GAVE ME
LOVE, TRADITION, AND THE COURAGE TO CREATE.
ANNIE

TO MY HEAVENLY FATHER WHOSE LOVING
KINDNESSES TOWARD ME ARE NEW EVERY MORNING.
JENA

• FAIRY BLESSINGS AND ROSES-A-BLOOM TO •
RUTH & RUSSELL BJORNSTAD, BURTON BERG, BONNIE STEWART
ZAN STEVENS, ANITA HAUSAFUS, & MR. GIL HODGES

ISBN 1-879244-35-7

FIRST EDITION
PRINTED IN MEXICO